What Are You
Waiting For?

Text copyright © 2003 by Cynthia L. Copeland
Illustrations copyright © 2003 by Mike Gordon

Reading Consultant: Lea M. McGee

Millbrook Press
A division of Lerner Publishing Group
241 First Avenue North
Minneapolis, Minnesota 55401 USA

Website address: www.lernerbooks.com

Library of Congress Cataloging-in-Publication Data

Copeland, Cynthia L.
What are you waiting for? / Cynthia L. Copeland ; illustrations by
Mike Gordon.
p. cm.—(Silly Millies)
Summary: A young boy, catching a glimpse of different construction
vehicles as they approach their work site, urges each to get busy.
ISBN-13: 978-0-7613-2804-9 (lib. bdg. : alk. paper)
ISBN-10: 0-7613-2804-1 (lib. bdg. : alk. paper)
ISBN-13: 978-0-7613-1828-6 (pbk. : alk. paper)
ISBN-10: 0-7613-1828-3 (pbk. : alk. paper)
[1. Construction equipment—Fiction.   2. Playgrounds—Fiction.]
I. Gordon, Mike, ill.   II. Title.   III. Series.
PZ7.C78793 Wh 2002   E]—dc21 2001007790

Manufactured in the United States of America
2 3 4 5 6 7 — DP — 10 09 08 07 06 05

silly Millies

What Are You Waiting For?

Cynthia L. Copeland
Illustrations by Mike Gordon

Turn
the
page!

M Millbrook Press • Minneapolis

What are you waiting for?

Hit it!

What are you waiting for?

Level it!

What are you waiting for?

Dump it!

What are you waiting for?

Drill away!

What are you waiting for?

Mix it!

What are you waiting for?

Build it!

NOW what are you waiting for?

Dear Parents:
Congratulations! By sharing this book with your child, you are taking an important step in helping him or her become a good reader. *What Are You Waiting For?* is perfect for the child who is learning the alphabet and getting ready to read.

TIPS FOR READING
- Before you read this book to your child, look through it together and talk about what's happening in the pictures. Then read the book aloud, pointing to the words as you read. It's a good idea to talk about the pictures as you read the book, making sure your child understands the connection between the words and the pictures. This will help your child move from being a passive listener to being an active reader!
- When you reread the book, see if your child will join you in saying a word or two from the text. This book was written with repeating words and phrases so that children can quickly join in the reading.
- After a few readings your child will know the book so well, he or she will be able to say the words from memory. Encourage your child to point to the words as he or she reads. Most of all, enjoy the funny story!

TIPS FOR DISCUSSION
- The boy in this story doesn't say much, but can your child try to imagine what he must be like? See if your child can make up a story about this boy. Is his dog his best friend? Is his Mom or Dad a construction worker? Does he want to have his birthday party at the new playground?
- In this book readers can predict what will happen next. Can your child predict what will happen now that the playground is built?

Lea M. McGee
University of Alabama
Tuscaloosa, AL